ACE VENTURA
PET DETECTIVE ™

PARROT IN PERIL

BY DEVRA NEWBERGER SPEREGEN
BASED ON THE SCREENPLAY BY STEVE ROBERTS

Troll

TM and © 1997 Morgan Creek Productions, Inc.
Published by Troll Communications L.L.C.

Printed in the United States of America. ISBN 0-8167-4334-7

10 9 8 7 6 5 4 3 2 1

Deep in the Amazon rain forest, three large bulldozers rumbled loudly, destroying everything in their path. The notorious Baron DeKlaw watched and smiled.

"Building resort hotels may be my business," he said to Mr. Brown, his assistant, "but destroying a wildlife habitat in the process is my *pleasure!*"

Suddenly, the bulldozers stopped. Something was in their way.

It was Ace Ventura, Pet Detective, and his monkey, Spike. They were sitting at a folding table playing chess!

"Who are you?" DeKlaw demanded.

Ace jumped up. "Name's Ace Ventura," he replied coolly, "sent by the Wildlife Protection League." He whipped out a map and stuck it in DeKlaw's face. "You can't build here. This land is a wildlife refuge."

"This land is owned by the DeKlaw Development Corporation," said the baron.

Ace whipped out more documents. "Oh, *reeheeheeheally?* Well, not according to *this* Endangered Species Report. And *this* court order! And *this* local map."

DeKlaw produced a map of his own. Ace looked it over. The map showed that the land was DeKlaw's.

But Ace was stubborn. "Well, alrighty!" he said. "But to keep going, you'll have to get past me first!" He tied himself to a tree right in front of the bulldozers.

DeKlaw smiled evilly. Then he told his men to cut down the tree and send it rolling down a big hill.

"You haven't seen the last of me!" cried Ace as he tumbled down the hill, into the river below.

"Excellent work, Mr. Brown," DeKlaw told his assistant. "That altered map looks completely legitimate. Even that Wildlife Protection League guy was fooled."

"When it comes to criminal conspiracy, Mr. DeKlaw, you're the best teacher!" said Brown.

"Altered map! Mr. Brown! Altered map!"

"Who said that?" DeKlaw asked. He gazed up into the trees. To his surprise, the voice was coming from a small parrot.

"Criminal conspiracy!" the parrot squawked. "Baron DeKlaw!"

DeKlaw gasped. "That parrot heard everything! If the information gets out, we're in trouble!" DeKlaw quickly detached the metal claw from his arm and snapped a machete knife in its place.

"After that parrot!" he ordered.

Later that day, Ace saw a small parrot examining a pile of fruit. Around the fruit was a rope trap. Holding the other end of the rope was none other than Baron DeKlaw.

Ace narrowed his eyes. *What does DeKlaw want with that parrot?* Sensing that something fishy was going on, Ace swung in and scooped up the parrot.

DeKlaw was furious. "It's Ace Ventura! He has our parrot. Follow him!"

DeKlaw and his men chased Ace until they came to a tent in
the forest. An old man with a bushy mustache jumped out to greet them. "Zee
name is Schweitzer! Dr. Schweitzer!" the man exclaimed in a thick accent.

DeKlaw eyed the doctor suspiciously. Then he looked around the side of the
tent. His gaze rested on a cot with a mysterious lump under its blanket. An
evil smile crept across his face. "Ventura! Now I've got you!" he exclaimed. With
his deadly knife hand he reached out and started to pull back the blanket.

"NO!!!" the doctor screamed, snatching the blanket back. "YOU HAVE JUST EXPOSED EVERYONE HERE TO ZEE DEADLY JUNGLE PLAGUE! VEE ALL HAVE JUST TWENTY SECONDS TO LIVE! Quick! Eat zeese leaves!" he said.

DeKlaw grabbed a handful and asked, while munching nervously, "What will these do?"

Dr. Schweitzer leaned in and whispered, "I'll show you." Then he reached inside his shirt and put a hand under his armpit. Bringing down his arm, he made a loud, crude *thwpt!*

DeKlaw's eyes widened. "You mean . . ."

"Yup! You *gassed* correctly!"

With a hearty "Heh-heh-heh-heh!" Ace ripped off his disguise and grabbed up Spike and the parrot from under the blanket. Then he ran from the tent. DeKlaw, doubled over with gas pains, couldn't chase after them.

"Say bye-bye, birdie, DeKlaw!" Ace called out.

High on a misty mountaintop at the border of the rain forest, Ace held the little parrot gently in his hands. "We may not have any evidence against DeKlaw," Ace proclaimed, "but at least we saved this parrot." Emotion overcame him. "Fly away and be free, my fine feathered friend!" He let go of the bird.

"Criminal conspiracy! Baron DeKlaw!" the parrot suddenly blurted out. Ace grabbed the parrot by the tail and pulled him back.

"Hold it right there! What did you say?"

The parrot spoke again. His voice sounded exactly like Baron DeKlaw's. "Even that Wildlife Protection League guy was fooled! *Squawk!* Excellent work, Mr. Brown! *Squawk!* The altered map looks completely legitimate!"

Ace snapped his fingers. "So *that's* what DeKlaw is up to! He changed the map!"

The parrot pulled away from Ace and flew off. Ace took a deep breath and adjusted the collar of his shirt. "Spike, we have to get that bird back!"

Ace and Spike scaled huge cliffs in the Kingdom of Parrots and trudged through the Mist of Forgetfulness in search of the parrot.

"Alrighty," Ace said as they climbed. "Here's the plan, Spike. We find that parrot, charter a plane to Washington, D.C., the bird testifies before a grand jury, and we put that Freddy Krueger wanna-be away for good!"

"Excellent work, Mr. Brown! *Squawk!* That altered map looks completely legitimate!"

Ace stopped dead in his tracks. The parrot! He pulled a flashlight from his back pocket and headed into the mouth of a dark cave. "Here, birdie, birdie," he called.

Seconds later, he emerged from the cave, parrot in hand.
Spike applauded.

"Dang, I'm good!" Ace gushed, with an ostrich-like
stretch of his neck.

But Ace's celebration was cut short when a sudden gust of wind knocked him off his feet. Before he knew what was happening, a helicopter appeared over his head. A cage dropped down from the copter and snatched the parrot. Ace looked up and saw Baron DeKlaw reeling in the cage. He shook a fist at the villain and screamed at the top of his lungs.

"DEKLAAAA . . ."

". . . AAAAAWWWWW, you loser!"

Ace grinned as the helicopter flew off. "I knew DeKlaw was following us," he explained to Spike, "so I threw him a decoy!" He went back into the cave and came out with another parrot.

"Criminal conspiracy! *Squawk!*" the parrot cried. Ace smiled again. DeKlaw had fallen for the oldest trick in the book—the ol' switcheroo!

Meanwhile, DeKlaw was wrapping his claw hand around the decoy parrot's neck. "You've sung for the last time, parrot!"

Suddenly, the parrot squawked. "Sixteen men on a dead man's chest! Yo ho ho and a bottle of rum!"

DeKlaw's jaw fell open. His face turned an angry shade of purple. "This is the wrong parrot!" he yelled.

The next day, Ace went to the nearest airport with the real parrot in his bag. But no planes were going to Washington, D.C. So he took matters into his own hands. He boarded a small plane and immediately made a big scene in front of the passengers.

"You call this an in-flight meal?" he barked at the stewardess. He ripped open the aluminum food tray, and there was Spike playing dead. "Why, this monkey tartare is still *moving!*"

Horrified, the passengers fled the plane, all except for two that Ace hadn't noticed before—DeKlaw and Brown!

"How did you find us?" Ace demanded.

DeKlaw pulled the impostor parrot from his suitcase. "A little bird told me," he said casually.

"Charter a plane! *Squawk!* Washington, D.C."

"Stool pigeon!" Ace sneered at the impostor parrot.

"Looks like this will be a short trip for you, Mr. Ventura." DeKlaw laughed and turned away. Brown pushed Ace out the plane door.

Ace toppled onto the runway and watched as the plane took off. This was not going as planned. Somehow, he had to save that parrot and stop DeKlaw from destroying the rain forest!

Ace slid open the large door to an enormous airplane hangar. Inside was the king of all aircraft—the Stealth Bomber! Ace climbed aboard and gunned the massive engine. Then he lifted off. But the Stealth was in reverse—and burst through the back wall of the hangar!

Ace searched the rain forest for the other plane. Finally, he spotted it in the distance. With Spike clinging nervously to his back, he pushed open the Stealth's cockpit cover and hopped onto the wing. With the Stealth right over the other plane, Ace jumped onto it and whipped open the door. Inside, several stewardesses and passengers stopped what they were doing and stared at Ace.

"A terrorist!" one of the passengers cried out.

"Huh?" Ace gulped. And before he could say, "Whoops, wrong plane," Ace was thrown off it.

Luckily, Ace and Spike landed on a snowy mountain. From there they could see yet another plane headed toward them. "*That* must be DeKlaw. But how are we going to get aboard?" Ace needed a plan.

Just then, a mountain climber arrived at the top of the mountain. "I've done it!" he cried joyously. "The first man ever to climb Mount—" Then he noticed Ace, lifted his snow goggles, and stared in disbelief.

"Actually, me and my monkey were first," Ace corrected him. "But no one needs to know our little secret—*if* you lend me your gear." The mountain climber quickly handed Ace some rope and a large hook.

In the plane, DeKlaw held his claw hand under the parrot's tiny throat. "I'm only going to say this one more time," he growled impatiently. "SPEAK!"

The parrot blinked a few times, then opened its beak. "Conspiracy!" it squawked. "Altered map! Looks legitimate!"

"It's him all right," DeKlaw said. "Eliminate him."

"Not so fast, DeKlaw!" a voice called out. DeKlaw whirled around.

"It's me, DeKlaw! And have you met my new little buddy?" Ace reached into his bag and whipped out Spike disguised as a squirrel with rabies— bushy tail, foamy mouth, the works. DeKlaw paled at the sight and began to sputter with fright. It was a pack of rabid squirrels that had chewed off his hand.

Ace snatched the parrot from DeKlaw and raced toward the airplane door. He pulled a parachute pack off the wall and shot DeKlaw a smug smirk.

"Hasta la vista . . . babieees!"

Ace turned to go. But before he could jump, Brown waved a cracker at the parrot. "Polly want a cracker?" To Ace's dismay, the parrot flew toward the snack.

DeKlaw smiled. "I'll keep the parrot, Mr. Ventura." He shoved Ace out the door. "Bon voyage! Again!"

"Heh-heh-heh-heh!"

DeKlaw's eyes grew wide. He knew that annoying laugh! It was Ventura! But how? He'd pushed him off the plane himself! He peered out the window and saw Ace holding on to the wing.

"Can't get rid of me that easily, DeKlaw!" Ace cried. "I'm like Jockey shorts on a hot summer day. . .all sweaty and clinging like the devil!"

DeKlaw was furious. He switched his claw hand for a saw and began sawing at the wing of the plane. The plane took a nosedive. The pilot ran out of the cockpit, strapped on a parachute, and jumped. Brown grabbed another chute and followed him. DeKlaw and Ace were alone now. And Ace had the last parachute.

DeKlaw stumbled onto the damaged wing. "Give me that chute!" he ordered.

"Yeah, right!" Ace said with a laugh.

DeKlaw lunged at Ace just as the plane nosedived again. Ace lost his grip on the parachute as he, DeKlaw, Spike, and the parrot were all thrown from the plane. Spike managed to catch the parachute and pull the cord. Ace grabbed on to the open chute, and the parrot landed safely on top of it. DeKlaw disappeared into the foliage below.

"*Monumental!*" Ace declared as he floated safely to the ground. "*Loo-hoo-hoo-ser!*"

A few days later, Ace stood on another mountaintop, holding the parrot. "You've seen much, my feathered *compadre*," he said. "Not every parrot gets to do the White House tour. So fly proud! Your testimony against DeKlaw helped save the rain forest, and now you can go!"

After a final hug, Ace let go of the parrot. The bird flapped its wings and started to fly away, but then blurted out a few parting words.

"Mr. President, I am in possession of classified information that could change the face of the world as we know it. *Squawk!*"

Ace and Spike exchanged wide-eyed looks. Then, quick as lightning, Ace snatched back the bird. "Here we go again!" he said.